Survival Ste & Benji: A South West Survival Story

Author: Chloe Kelly & Steven Kelly

Illustrator: Adam Endacott

Copyright © 2021

On a warm, bright summers day, Survival Ste
and Benji the toy poodle went on a quest.

They entered the deep, dark forest and strolled until they
could find a place to set up camp. Twigs were snapping,
vines were shaking and the wind was whistling.

Eventually, they found a perfect spot with birds tweeting
and in cover from the wind. Survival Ste set up camp
and prepared some nettle tea.

**STEVEN'S SURVIVAL TIPS**

Collect nettle leaves, add
water and heat to a near
boil. Use two cups of water
for a cup of leaves. Once
the water is near boiling,
reduce heat and simmer
for a couple minutes.

Survival Ste was shocked, and worried for Benji.

As the adventure went on Survival Ste came across a large swamp of courageous crocodiles snapping their mighty jaws.

Survival Ste had no time to waste.

SWOOSH!

He lunged to the trees and used the vines to swing across the swamp.

Suddenly there was a loud hiss!
ACK!
Survival Ste then realised he had swung from a slimy snake!
Z Z Z
Z Z Z

Survival Ste entered
a narrow, dark and
gloomy cave.

With no torch to hand Ste had to make something to give himself some light.

Using his flint and steel, some material and a tree branch he made a fire torch.

CHH
CHH
CHH

While roaming the cave, Survival Ste had to fend off scuttling scorpions, curious spiders and creepy crawlies!

HISSSS!!

After a cold, long and wet walk through the cave,
Ste found the exit and set up camp next to a river.

## STEVEN'S SURVIVAL TIPS

Find a green branch/stick.
...
For Fuel, you can use
neutral (tree resin, bark) or
manmade (Kerosene, gas,
lighter fluid) materials.
...
Wrap a cloth around
the end of the stick.
...
If using a manmade
accelerant, soak the cloth
for a few minutes before
lighting.
...
Light your torch!

Survival Ste was getting hungry so he caught some fish and roasted them over the fire. All he could think about was his best friend, Benji the toy poodle.

In the morning, as the weather was raging and the trees were whistling, Survival Ste was determined to find Benji the toy poodle - nothing was going to stop him.

**STEVEN'S SURVIVAL TIPS**

A simple hook and line, along with some bait is really all you need to catch fish. Hand lines are usually handheld coils of line that are cast and retrieved by hand.

Before he set off, he used the shadow stick method to get his direction, then carried on with his quest.

## LEARN THE SHADOW STICK METHOD

1. Place a straight stick in the ground in a sunny area.

2. Place a rock where the stick's shadow ends. This marks West.

3. Wait 10-15 minutes. The shadow will have moved.

4. Place another rock at the end of the new shadow placement. This marks East.

5. Draw a line or place a stick between the two rocks.

6. Add another line/stick perpendicular to the previous line. This represents true North and South!

To his delight he came across something very familiar.

"Is that Benji's footprint?" he shouted with excitement. He now knew he was going in the right direction.

Suddenly, he came across his map in a muddy puddle, along with a muddy paw print trail!

15

# TIME FOR
# SOME FUN
# ACTIVITIES!

| Help Survival Ste find these words: | TORCH TENT SUPPLIES SKILL | MAP ROPE WATER BOOTS | COAT BENJI STEVEN |
|---|---|---|---|

| A | T | O | R | C | H | F | P | S | O |
|---|---|---|---|---|---|---|---|---|---|
| E | M | B | O | O | T | S | E | K | O |
| R | H | J | S | A | E | U | H | I | R |
| B | P | T | L | T | R | P | S | L | B |
| E | W | L | E | Q | Z | P | A | L | O |
| N | A | S | H | N | T | L | W | Y | O |
| J | T | O | O | A | T | I | J | M | J |
| I | E | H | E | L | B | E | H | A | E |
| O | R | O | P | E | S | S | N | P | O |
| R | E | S | T | E | V | E | N | B | S |

**Colour in
Survival Ste**

**Colour in Benji**

# MEET THE
# AUTHORS

## CHLOE & STEVEN KELLY

Steven is a full time soldier serving in the 29 Commando Regiment Royal Artillery based in Plymouth. His daughter Chloe is 12 years old and a dancer. Chloe was inspired to write this book due to all of the adventures with Benji told to her by Steven.

# THE REAL LIFE
# STE & BENJI

Benji accompanies Steven on many of his in real life journeys and is always the ever faithful companion.

You can follow their ongoing adventures on social media!

 @Survival_Ste

# MEET THE ILLUSTRATOR

## ADAM ENDACOTT

Adam Endacott is an illustrator and graphic designer, born and raised in Plymouth, Devon.

With a BA (Hons) degree in Illustration from the Plymouth College of Art, work experience at Hallmark Cards, and a strong visual style, you can have full peace of mind knowing your story is in safe hands.

Adam was extremely honored to be given the task of adapting this story into a visual format and help people learn new skills in this medium!

If you would like to hire Adam to visualise your story, or for any illustration work in general, get in touch!

 **Adam Endacott**

 **Adam Endacott Illustrations**

 **@adam_endacott**

 **@AdamEndacott**